Contents

Chapter 1

I've been laying in bed for the past hour. I just have this feeling like something bad is going to happen. Today is my 19th birthday you'd think I would be happy. I'm not really big on my birthday, part of that could be that my mom died the day after my birthday. Liza was supposed to come over today for my birthday but she had to go visit her grandma in the nursing home. It's okay though I understand her grandma hasn't been doing very well. I hope she is doing better. Well I guess I better get up.

I went to take a shower and brush my teeth. When I was done I went to pick out my clothes for today (outfit at the top of the page). I put on some mascara and chapstick and I was done. Winter should be home she's always trying some kind of new recipe in the kitchen. Winter is great she has taken care of me since my mother died. She was one of her friends. I don't know much about my mother she died when I was 4 I don't remember her though. All I have is a picture winter gave me in a locket when I turned 7. Winter is great but she's not really like a mom she's more like that fun aunt you spend the summer with.

I walked downstairs to the kitchen expecting to find winter there like always. But she wasn't I was about to call out for her when I noticed a note on the fridge. I picked it up.

Dear, GidgetI'm so sorry for leaving and not telling you. Just know that I had to leave for my own safety and yours. I know none of this will make sense right now but tonight at midnight everything will change. There is a car waiting outside it will take you somewhere safe I promise. I can't protect you anymore but they can. I will see you again one day. Just know that I love you and please listen and be safe.

With love,Winter

This can't be right she wouldn't just leave me like that she's all I have. I don't know who any of my family is I don't even know who my father is. This has got be some kind of sick joke. Right? I rush upstairs grab my phone and purse and go outside to test my theory. When I walk out I notice right away a black SUV with an older man in a suit standing beside it. I walked up to him.

"Are you Gidget?" He asked.

"Yes?" It came out more like a question when I said it.

He opened the car door for me to go in. Before I did I asked "where are you taking me?"

"Sorry miss but I was only told to pick you up and bring you there safely." He said.

"Okay." I whispered.Right now I don't really have anything to lose. I did something that is most likely the dumbest thing ever. I got in the car. I don't recognize anywhere we went past and after a while I fell asleep.

I woke up to someone gently shaking my shoulders. I rubbed my eyes and looked at who was disturbing my sleep. It was the driver.

"Miss we're here you need to wake up." He said kinda loud.

"Okay, okay I'm up." I said.

I got out of the car and followed the man whose name I still don't know. When I looked up my jaw dropped. This place is huge why would anyone want me here. It's more like a mansion than a house. I've never seen a place so big before. As I got to the front door, he held it open for me.

"Thank you." I said.

He nodded his head in acknowledgment and I went on in. It was beautiful on the inside just like the outside. There was a huge chandelier when you enter and past that was a rustic looking wood staircase. The man caught my attention when he started to walk again I followed closely behind. He took me to another room on the far left. He knocked on the door when we got to it.

"What?" A deep voice said it sounded emotionless and a little annoyed .

"Sir I have the girl you wanted me to pick up." The driver said.

"Bring her in." He said.

I walked in and almost gasped at the sight I saw. The man sitting at the desk was hot he had dark hair and beautiful blue eyes and tattoos that I could see where his white dress shirt was unbuttoned at the top and his sleeves rolled up. I stayed silent and waited for him to speak. I noticed I was staring and instantly look down at my feet. It was silent for a while I could feel him staring at me but I was too afraid to look up and meet his gaze.

Finally he spoke up and said "Jason will show you to your room, someone will come up to get you when it's dinner time. Your things will be here to-morrow. Stay in your room and don't go outside there will be bodyguards posted outside of your room. I will not answer your questions right now. Tomorrow we will talk for now go."

He said it with great authority. I stayed silent and walked out to find the driver who I now know his name is Jason. Jason walked up the stairs to the first door on the right and stopped. I walked in it was huge the room was dark with accents of red in places. There was a big queen sized bed with a black canopy at the top. There was a bay window with a bench and pillows on it. I loved it. I can't wait to read in that window.

This room is great but not great enough to be trapped in it all day. I guess I have a long time to wait. I walked to the small desk in the corner of the room and noticed a pencil and paper on it. I take them to the window and sit and draw for a while. The view is great I can see a huge flower garden with a fountain and a pond in the middle. I wish I could go outside to see it better. Maybe tomorrow I can bring that up when I talk to him again. I just hope I make it through today.

Chapter 2

<hr>

After I sat at the window for I don't know how long drawing I heard a knock on the door. I got up and walked across the room to the door and opened it. There was a girl in a maid uniform standing there.

"Miss it's time for dinner. Oh! And these are for you to sleep in since you won't have your things till tomorrow." She said softly and handed me the clothes looked like black and white t-shirt and sweatpants.(picture at the top)

"Thank you." I replied.

"Your welcome Miss." she said then started to walk.

I followed her downstairs to the dining room. It was large with a big rectangle dark wood dining table and matching chairs. There had to be at least enough seats for 20 or more people. There was a large chandelier hanging above the middle of the table. I was so distracted by the beautiful room I didn't even notice he was sitting at the end of the table. He's looking straight at me I avert my eyes to the floor and sit a seat away from him. That's a safe distance, right? I think so, oh well. He didn't say anything. So I took it upon myself to start a conversation or at least try to.

"Um... mr... uh. sorry what's your name?" I stammered a little.

With an unamused look on his face he replied "Xavier."

"Xavier I wanted to ask you a question." I stated "um... well... I was wondering if maybe I could... uh."

"Are you going to get to the point or keep stuttering around." He said coldly.

"I wanted to know if I can go into the garden one day." I said. I'm tired of trying to be nice when he is so rude to me.

"No." He replied."What? Why?""Because I said no. It's for your own safety."

"I don't understand what's so dangerous about going into a garden. What am I even hiding from." I said louder this time. "Why won't anybody tell me what the hell is going on. I've lived a normal life for 19 years and all of the sudden I'm in danger. It doesn't make any sense!" I was practically yelling at this point.

He stood up from his seat in an instant. "This is my house and you will do as I say. Your lucky I even agreed to help protect you. If it wasn't for the fact winter saved my life once long ago I would have never agreed to it! I don't want you here anymore than you want to be here and I most certainly have much better things to do than this!" He yelled

That last part hurt even though I'm not sure why I mean I only just met the man. He walked out of the room passing one of the cooks on the way.

He turned and said "bring me a plate to my office." With that he left and walked to his office. I heard the door slam I jumped a little at how loud the sound was. A moment later a cook came out with two plates of food. She sat one in front of me. It had fried chicken, mashed potatoes, corn, and a roll. My favorite meal, weird. I looked up as she walked out with the other plate she held it high so I couldn't really see it but there wasn't any food sticking up to see. I guess he wasn't very hungry. But I am so I grabbed my fork and dug in. I finished all my food. Ugh, geez I'm stuffed now. I think I ate too much I can't move.

After a few minutes I started to walk upstairs and to my room. I heard a noise come from Xavier's office I stopped for a moment to see what it was. Silence was all that followed so I went on to my room. I got the clothes the maid gave me and went to the bathroom which by the way was almost half as big as the room. I showered, brushed my teeth, and braided my hair. When I walked back into the room I grabbed my phone to check the time. 10:49pm so I went on to bed. Darkness soon followed and I fell asleep.

I awoke in the middle of the night broke out in a sweat all over. Felt like every muscle in my body was on fire. Then pain ripples through my body and I couldn't take it anymore I screamed. I've never felt pain this bad before. I couldn't move I felt too weak. I was shaking and then the pain came back and I screamed again. Someone came in and said "It's happening." That's the last thing I heard before everything went dark.

When I woke up again the pain was gone but I still felt weak. I tried to move but someone stopped me. I opened my eyes and my brown ones were met with striking blue ones. I realized I was staring and averted my eyes. He was touching my arm. It felt like little sparks of electricity everywhere his hand was touching. I looked back up and met his gaze again his eyes were wide like he was shocked about something. The emotion was soon covered up with his usual emotionless expression. He jerked his hand back as if he was burnt. Then said, "You need to rest I will explain after you rest more." With that he walked out. After a while my eyes started to get droopy. Soon after fell asleep.

I woke up to someone talking. "I know but she needs to know. You can't keep it from her any longer. Your not protecting her anymore I am and I can't do that very well if she doesn't even know why she needs protected." Xavier said sounding quite annoyed with whoever he was one the phone with.

He turned towards me and noticed I was awake. "I've got to go she's awake but this conversation is not over." He said walking over to my bed as he hung up the phone.

"How do you feel?" He said. Well that wasn't what I expected. "I feel fine a little weak but I'm okay." I replied."Do you know what happened last night?""No.""I'm going to tell you something but I need to promise to let me finish explaining and not interrupt me." He said calmly. "Okay."

"There are things that you can never imagine in this world. They've been here for centuries and are more dangerous than you may think. You need to understand the world you know is about to completely change. Vampires are real and Gidget you're a vampire, your mother & father where vampires. Winter is a witch and she cast a spell on you and your mother when you were born. The spell made it to where you appear human and have human qualities, it made it to where you were undetectable to any vampire you were just a normal human. Only thing is that's a very powerful spell so it will only work for a short matter of time when you turned 19 the spell started to wear off. At midnight you turned into a full vampire. You will need to cope with your urges and learn how to control your abilities. The reason your so weak is because you need to feed. You need blood." He explain

I stared at him wide eyed. I started to get up to leave. These people are crazy, nuts. Has to be some kinda weird cult or something. I just want to go home and be normal.i headed to the door. He was in front of me in a flash. I looked back then to him. How did he do that? Whatever, I'm probably just imagining things. I reach for the handle but he stops me standing in front of the door.

"You can't leave." Xavier said."And why not?""I just explained to you why not.""Your crazy if you believe any of that.""Okay I'll prove it to you.""Oh, really and how do you plan on doing that?"

He opened his mouth and there were fangs. Have those always been there? I don't know, he never smiles so it's possible. I cross my arms over my chest and lean in. They look real. I lift my hand and touch one It pricks my finger making a drop of blood appeared. Oh! No I'm not good with blood. Black spots started to appear. I felt dizzy then everything went black and I fell to the floor only to be caught in strong arms.

Chapter 3

When I woke up there was an IV in my arm with what looked like blood, I started to feel queasy so I turned away from it before I faint again. After a few minutes I started to feel okay again. I was feeling better than earlier. I laid there for a moment then I realized what had happened before I fainted. Either I'm nuts or that was all a dream. I mean vampires aren't real that's just ridiculous. Right? It's impossible, surely people would notice if there were vampires and witches. If it's true then what else is out there that I don't know about. Oh my God what if unicorns are real. Man I hope unicorns are real.

I have a bigger problem right now though, cause if I'm a vampire won't I die? I can't drink blood I faint every time, I can't stand to see my own blood let alone drink from someone or something. I kept my head turned and pulled out the IV from my arm. I got up and started pacing trying to think of anything I could possibly do. Then I saw it a drop of blood on the floor. My knees went weak instantly and I fell toward the floor. I heard someone open the door and in an instant caught me before I was on the floor.

"Woah, what are you doing out of bed?" Xavier asked"I was just thin king.""You're still too weak to be walking around." He almost sounded concerned, almost being the key word.

"Am I going to die?" I asked with a quiet voice."Why would you die?" He replied"Because I can't drink blood, don't I need it to survive?""Well, yes but you haven't even tried to drink blood. You will just have to work on it .""But I faint every time, even thinking about it makes me nauseous.""Why are you afraid of blood?" He asked"I don't know." I whisper "There must be a reason, some kind of experience in the past.""I don't know, I've been this why since I can remember." I stated. "When I was little I remember Winter had to distract me when the doctor took my blood. I would get sick every time. I used to cry then I would get so dizzy I passed out."

"I think you may have some kind of repressed memories if you could access them then maybe you could get over this fear of yours." He stated before walking to the door. "Get some rest tomorrow Stephen will start to teach you about being a vampire."

"Why can't you just teach me?" I mumbled low enough I thought he wouldn't hear.

"Because I have more important things to do then babysit a vampire that's afraid of blood." He said coldly then walked out. I felt a pang in my heart. I don't know why I feel horrible why would I care what he thinks. I just met him and he's been nothing but rude. I thought with our conversation earlier maybe he would open up some. Guess not he wants to be rude then so can I.

I got out of bed and went to put my clothes on for today (picture at the top). When I was done showering and getting dressed I peaked out of my door to see if anyone was there. There wasn't any guards like he said. Which means either he lied or they thought I was to weak to leave. Sucks for them. Haha sucks, cause there vampires. I walk out of the room towards the stairs being careful and listening for anyone. It's silent so rush down quietly and make a break for the door. I turn the knob slowly. It opens. Yes! I rush out of the house and make my way to the back making sure there aren't any windows that someone might see me through. In the garden it's gorgeous. It's so green it almost looks fake, with huge white roses in the front and neatly trimmed hedges guarding the sides of the garden. When I entered I notice the rock pathway and followed it. It lead past all the beautiful variations of white and red flowers. I finally reached the pond in the middle with a statue of a woman with fountain forming at the skirt of her dress. Her eyes were covered by her hand and when I looked closer it looked like more water came from her eyes to form tears. It was absolutely tragically beautiful.

This was most definitely my new favorite pace. I went through the rest of the garden looking ant all the different flowers and colors. It was starting to get dark I hadn't noticed it was that late. I went to turn back but realized that I was completely lost. I kept making turns but I never made it to the exit. It's too dark to see. I start to feel really weak I'm not sure why. My knees start to give out and I just lay on the ground not having the will to move. I don't know how long I was there like that but right before I slipped into the darkness I heard someone. "Found her sir." He said.

I smelt something amazing, I can't really describe it. I've never smelt something like it before. I felt something wet against my lips. A drop passed through and then I couldn't get enough. I opened my eyes and I couldn't believe what I saw, there was a girl in a maid uniform with her bloody wrist pressed against my mouth. I felt a wave of nausea pass through me as I broke out in a cold sweat all over. I turn to the side where thank God there was a trash can and threw up all the contents of my stomach. I was so tired after, I fell asleep again. I awoke to someone talking I could just barely hear them.

"What's wrong with her?" Xavier asked"Well if it's like you said and she's afraid of blood this is a very common reaction." The doctor replied. "Though I've never known a vampire to have these symptoms, my best guess would be a traumatic past event for being the cause.""I know that much but how do you fix it?" He asked. "If she keeps this up she'll be dead by next week." Xavier stated"My suggestion would be to do a memory search with her, since you are mate it should work successfully. She needs to face her past before anything else.

Mates? Like friends? He's not my friend I barely know him. He hates me I'm pretty sure. So why does he want to help. "Probably for Winter." I thought grimly.

"Sir she's awake." The doctor said"Then why hasn't she opened her eyes?" He said"She's in a coma like state, you need to do the memory search with her before she loses conciseness again." He said. "If not then I'm afraid you may lose her sooner than next week.""Okay, how do I do it?" Xavier asked

What the hell are they going to do. This memory search thing sounds weird. Will he see them I don't want him to. He doesn't even like me. I need to move. I can't feel my body. Well I guess I get no say in this even though it's my memories.

"Your going to have to feed from her""NO!"

"You have to if you want to save her." The doctor said."I can't, what if I lose control?" He sounded concerned."You don't need much it shouldn't come to that.""Okay."

"Then you must give her your blood. Then cut both your forearms and press them together and it should begin." The doctor directed Xavier.

I felt something at my neck. No! I don't want to be bitten. It's going to hurt and the blood. I felt something sharp then he bite me. It felt like nothing else. It didn't hurt at all, it felt ... good. As soon as it can it was gone. Something wet pressed against my lips. A drop slipped through, it tasted sweet. Even better than the blood from before. That was all I got, I felt a little disappointed. I wanted more. I felt different almost like I could sense that he was there beside me. I felt something slice through my forearm. Then quickly something was pressed against it.

In an instant I was back to the day I tried so hard to forget. The day after my birthday when I just turned 4. The day my mother died. I could see the young me playing in the kitchen with my mom. We were baking cupcakes. I was putting sprinkles on the icing when the doorbell rang. I looked up at my mom she signaled me to be quiet by putting her finger to her lips. Then pointed to the cabinet under the sink. I went to it to hide. I was so scared I didn't know what was happening. I had it crack so I could see some. I could hear my mom and some man screaming at each other.

"DO YOU KNOW HOW LONG I WAITED FOR YOU!" The man screamed at her."I HAD TO LEAVE, YOU NEVER LOVED ME. PROBABLY WERE WITH ONE OF YOUR WHORES THE SEC-OND I LEFT!" Mom yelled back."You shouldn't have run away." He said coldly."Why cause you'll beat me, you already did that for years."

I couldn't we his face, only from the torso down same with my mom. He came closer towards her, she backed up until she was against the refriger-ator. He kept getting closer until he was right in front of her.

"STOP!" Mom screamedHe pulled something out of his pocket and stabbed her in the stomach. Tears were streaming down my face as I covered my eyes. I could still hear her screams and the stabs. I was shaking I just want it to end. The man stated muttering something to himself and walk away I wasn't a while after I heard the door shut. I came out of hiding and ran over to her.

"MOMMY!" I screamed while running I almost feel, there was blood everywhere. The one white kitchen was painted with red. Her eyes weren't opening. Why won't they open.

"Mommy wake up." I cried into her."Please.""Mommy!" I sobbed louder

I laid there with her for I don't know how long crying. I heard the doorbell ring but I wasn't leaving her I couldn't.

"Hey you guys left the door unlocked. Where are you?" I heard winter say.

I heard footsteps getting closer, then a gasp. She ran up to me and pulled me into a hug.

"Gidget are you okay? He didn't hurt you did he?" She asked I shook my head as a reply I couldn't talk I would just cry even more. "Did he see you?"I shook my head again"I need to get you out of here okay?""No!" I yelled now crying again. "I can't leave her here!" I sobbed clinging to her lifeless body."We have to they are going to be back and I won't let you die too." She said strictly.

She pulled me away from mom and to her. I cried into her shirt as she ran out of the house taking me with her.

I came to and had strong arms holding me tightly to his chest as I cried into his shirt .I could tell it was Xavier, I felt the little sparks spread across my skin. I felt calmer with him holding me. Then it left, he go up so quickly you'd think I burnt him. He didn't say anything he just rush out of the room. What I do he was being so nice then so rude the next moment. I swear he's bipolar. I pulled my knees to my chest and silently cried. After a while I started to fall asleep so I laid down and let the darkness take over.

I awoke with a sharp pain in my chest. The pain spread all over I couldn't take it any longer I screamed, my vains felt like they were on fire. It hurt so bad I started clawing at my chest to make it stop but blacked out shortly after.

~~~

Authors note
~~~

A lot happened in this chapter let me know what you think so far.

~ Sadie

2094 words

Chapter 4

After what felt like forever the pain finally subsided. I lay there feeling completely drained emotionally and physically. I fell asleep and didn't wake up until almost 11:00am. I got up did my morning routine which consisted of a shower, brushing my teeth, drying my hair and getting dressed(outfit at the top). I curled my hair and put a little make up on and went downstairs. I still felt like crap but hopefully the makeup help me not look like I feel. I went to the kitchen. It was nice with white countertops and black cabinets. When I came in there was a girl looking inside the fridge. She was wearing the shirt Xavier had on yesterday. I remember the blue from when I cried on it, it even still had a smug from my tears. I turned my head and cleared my throat.

She turned around towards me her red curled hair bounced a little. Her brown eyes met with mine, she was pretty and tall at least 5'8. Which compared to my 5'2 seemed very tall.

"Who are you?" She sneered."I'm Gidget." I stated "Who are you?""I'm Bianca, Xavier's girlfriend." She said proudly."Oh." For some reason that didn't sit well with me."Why are you even here?" She asked in a harsh voice."I honestly don't know, no one will tell me.""You must be the reason Xavier has been so busy recently."

She came closer to me she pointed at my chest and said "You better stay away from Xavier cause he's mine. Got it."

I pushed her hand away and pushed her back some."First of all I don't want Xavier, second I don't even want to be here but I sure as hell am not going to listen to anything some whore tells me to do. You're not the boss of me, I don't even know you. So get out of my face and go bug Xavier." I'm so sick of everyone just walking all over me, I tried to be nice but I'm done now. I walked to the counter grabbed an apple and got a water from the fridge, this will do for now.

With that I left and went out to the garden to eat. I still feel so weak I might pass out but I can't drink blood yet. I don't think I would faint again but the thought makes me sick still. Everytime I close my eyes I see my mom lying there covered in her own blood. Whoever did that to her is still out there. Maybe that's who their protecting me from. Why would anyone want to kill my mother? I want answers and I want them now, no one will tell me anything I just want someone to be honest with me for once.When I'm done eating I go back in the house and I hear yelling.

"WHERE THE HELL IS SHE!" Xavier roared."I DON'T KNOW, HOW MANY TIMES DO I HAVE TO TELL YOU!" Bianca yelled back."You were the only one down here and you had an argument with her, so forgive me if I don't see you as the victim in this situation." He sneered."SHE CALLED ME A WHORE!" She screeched at him."THAT'S BECAUSE YOU ARE ONE!""I'M YOUR GIRLFRIEND!""NO! YOU'RE NOT, I'VE TOLD YOU BEFORE I DON'T DO RELATIONSHIPS!"

"But""No." He interrupted. "She's my mate she had every right to say those things to you if not more.""S..She's your mate." She stammered."Yes." He said in a low voice."But we...""I know.""Are you rejecting her then?""No."

"What?why?" She squeaked."Cause I don't want to, not to mention with her in this state she would most likely die.""Wasn't she in pain last night though?" She said sounded almost happy."Yes." He stated through clenched teeth."Okay, well can we do that again?" She said in a fake sweet voice."No that was a mistake.""What?""You heard me now leave or you will be forced to leave." He said strictly.

She huffed and stormed out of his office right into me, pushed me aside and went out the front door. I went into his office and closed the door determined to get some answers from him. He took a drink from his glass on the desk as he looked up at me with wide eyes.

"What are mates? Cause we aren't friends, and I don't understand why that would even come between you and your girlfriend." I askedHe choked on his drink a little before replying "it's nothing." He stated."It's something if you and your girlfriend argued about it.""She's not my girlfriend." He said loudly."Okay but still, what are mates?""Fine, you really want to know?"I nodded

"Okay, mates are soulmates, the one person you're supposed to be with forever. The person you were made for. You can tell who your mate is by the sparks you feel when you touch them. The more you're around your mate the stronger the bond gets. To complete the bond both mates must mark each other. Once it's completed you can read each other's thoughts and sense their presence. If the bond is established and a mate cheats it causes the other one pain." He explained.

So that's why it hurt so much last night. He knew it would hurt me and he did it anyway. He doesn't care about me, he doesn't care about anyone but himself. I started to back away as he approached me.

"You hurt me.""I know""How do you reject a mate?"He turned to me with a furious look. "You will not reject me, I made a mistake it won't happen again. You don't understand I don't do relationships I haven't for centuries. I started to feel for you and got scared." He said coming towards me. I Backed up till I hit a wall. "I promise it won't happen again""How do I know that you'll keep it?""I guess you'll just have to trust me.""Yah, cause that's gone great for me so far." I said sarcastically.

He smiled brought his hand up to my cheek brushing his knuckles against it. I felt sparks spread across my cheek as I closed my eyes and leaned into his touch. I opened my eyes and saw the most beautiful smile ever. I've never seen him smile. I smile back looking up at him. He looked at me confused."What?" He said softly."Nothing I've just never seen you smile before." I said brushing my fingertips across his lips. " I like it." That made him smile again.

He started to lean in, my eyes went wide and a little panicked. I've never kissed anyone before but when his lips met mine all the worry went away. I melted into his arms slowly bringing my hands to his hair as he deepened the kiss. I felt sparks all over it was like I was floating. He pulled away and stared into my brown eyes like he was searching for something. I smiled up at him, he smiled even bigger than before. I felt so bubbly now. When he started to walk back to his desk I started to feel dizzy. I lost my balance and leaned forward reaching for one of the chairs but missed. As I fell to the floor Xavier was there in a flash and caught me.

He held my head up and said "we need to get you blood now."

I shook my head no but he picked me up and carried me to my bed. He got to his phone and called someone. A minute later a maid came in. She sat on the bed next to me and put her wrist up to my mouth. I hesitantly looked up at Xavier, he nodded his head. I bit into her arm, instantly my throat felt like it was on fire. I pushed her wrist away. I felt bile rise in the throat I turned my head and reached for the trash can throwing up the blood in the bin. Xavier rushed to me. I felt worse than before I closed my eyes and fell into the darkness. When I woke up I heard talking.

"Why can't she keep the blood down? She's going to die." Xavier said"Well maybe she just can't keep human blood down. She didn't throw up your blood did she?" The doctor from before said."No, she didn't throw it up.""Try again then."

I heard them come through the door. Xavier touched my shoulder a shook it lightly. I opened my eyes and looked up at him. He put his wrist to my mouth but I shook my head.

"You have to it's your only chance. Please I only just got you I can't lose you."I looked up once more before biting down on his wrist. It tasted as amazing as before, almost addictive. After a while I felt him start to pull away but I held him in place. However he pulled me off.

"That's enough for now. Go ahead a rest more, I'll see you tomorrow."

I nodded my head too tired to talk. I leaned back and fell back asleep.

~~~

A/NSo they had their first kiss. Not sure if she let him off the hook to easy or not. Anyone think Xavier will mess it up again? Let me know.

~ Sadie

1592 words
~~~

Chapter 5

---

1 week later

I felt someone shaking me. I groaned and turned away from the horrid person that dared disturb my peaceful sleep. Ugh, they won't stop. Can't they take a hint.

"Go away." I mumbled tiredly."Come on love, wake up." Xavier said."It's too early.""It's 10:30am."

"That's too early come back in an hour and a half." I said."O-kay, I guess I just won't show you my surprise." He said.I was instantly intrigued, "Surprise?" I asked.

" Yah but you don't want to know so I'll just go now." He said heading towards the door.I practically jumped out of bed. "No! Wait, I'm up." I said in a rushed voice.He walked over to me and smiled. "Okay, get dressed and meet me downstairs."

He kissed my forehead and walked out the door. I walked to the bathroom to shower and get ready. I dried my hair and braided it, then got dressed(outfit at the top). I left and headed downstairs, as I descended the stairs I got to thinking about how much Xavier has opened up to me this past week. He told me about how his parents were killed when he was 10 and that was when Winter saved his life. He didn't go into detail but I could tell it was a hard subject for him so I didn't press the subject. He told me about how he was raised by his best friend Stephen's parents and how the only people he trusts is his sister, Stephen and his parents, and Landon. We've come so far in just a week. I can feel it through the bond too, it's like I can feel what he's feeling now.

When I got to the bottom of the stairs I saw Xavier talking with two guys by the door. One was blonde and the other had fiery red hair. When Xavier noticed me he smiled and motioned for me to come over. I went and stood next to him looking up at the other two men as they also smiled at me.

"Stephen & Landon, this is Gidget my mate." Xavier said "Gidget this is Stephen." Pointing to the blonde guy. "And this is Landon." Pointing to the redhead. "Nice to meet you both." I smiled and waved awkwardly.S uddenly I was brought into a hug. "Nice to meet you too Gidget." They both said and I couldn't help but laugh as they both hugged me.I was pulled out of the hug and into Xavier's arms. "She's my mate. Get your own."They both put their hands up in surrender as they started to was out."Bye Gidget." Stephen said."See ya Gidget."Landon said."Bye guys." I replied.

We walked outside and around the house towards the garden. Xavier put his hands over my eyes as he lead me to his surprise. After a little walking we stopped.

"Ready?" He asked.I nodded my head.

He removed his hand. We were in the garden by the fountain but now there was a beautiful bench sat in front of it. I stared at it with wide eyes. He did this for me? No ones ever done something so thoughtful for me. My eyes got a little glossy as I turned to him. His smile fell when he saw my face."What's the matter? You don't like it?" He asked."I can get you different one if you want." He said.

I stood on my tiptoes and kissed him on the lips. When I pulled away I hugged him tightly and said, "I love it."I looked up at him and he smiled again."Why did you look like you were going to cry?""It's just no ones ever done something like this for me before." I said quietly and looking down at my feet.

"I noticed how you come out here everyday to this spot. Even though I've told you not to but I thought if you're going to do it, you should at least have a bench to sit on." He said."Thank you." I said sincerely.He raised his hand to my cheek and said, "No need to thank me, I wanted to do it.""My sister is coming by today and I would like for you to meet her.""I would love to.""We'll have dinner with her tonight then." He smiled."Sadly I must go work now but I will see you for dinner, Okay?" I nodded and he kissed my lips and headed out of the garden.

I sat on the bench for a little while enjoying the view before deciding to go back inside the house. I went up to my room and sat in the window to draw. I don't know how long it had been but I was getting bored with drawing. Since all of my stuff is here now so are my books I went over and grabbed one. City of Bones, one of my favorites. I decided to but the bench to good use and go to the garden to read. I walked out and went down the stairs. I could hear yelling coming from Xavier's office.

"WHY WON'T YOU LISTEN! HE'S NOT BAD! HE'S MY MATE AND I LOVE HIM!" That voice sounds familiar."I DON'T CARE HE HAS KILLED TO MANY OF HIS OWN KIND AND HE WOULDN'T HESITATE TO KILL YOU TOO!" Xavier roared."Just do this on thing for me, please." In a pleading voice.

It's Liza! How does she know Xavier.

"I'm sorry but I can't. He's too dangerous." He said."But I'm your sister. I just want this one thing." Liza said.

My eyes wide with surprise. Liza is his sister. She's a vampire she's been lying to me all these years. She's been my best friend for four years. Why would she do that to me. I don't know if I can ever trust her again. Xavier look up at me in surprise. Liza saw him and followed his gaze to me.

"Gidget?" She asked."You know my mate?" Xavier asked Liza.She nodded. He turned to me and asked, "How do you know her?""I don't know her, I thought I did, but I don't." I said as a tear streaked my right cheek.

I walked out of the office and ran up the stairs to my room I heard Liza yelling for me but I was already gone. When I reached the door I went in and locked. I sat in the window staring outside trying to think of why everyone seems to lie to me.

~~~

A/N

I would have had the chapter sooner but when I went back to it all that I had wrote was gone so I had to start all over. Hope you liked it let me know you thoughts so far. Did anyone predict that Liza was a vampire too?

~ sadie

1156 words
~~~

Chapter 6

I know that I need to talk to Liza and let her explain. Maybe she has a good reason for lying to me but she has lied to me for our entire friendship. All those times she went to see her grandma, was she really coming here? Why did she act like my friend for so long? Did Winter know too. I have all these questions but I'm not sure if I'm ready to talk to her yet. I can talk to her I don't have to decide to forgive her right away. Right? I heard knocking on my door but I ignored it.

"Gidget, I know you can hear me." He sighed, "Please, open up. It's just me."

I walked to the door. "Just you?" I said."Just me, I promise.""Okay." I said quietly before opening the door slowly.

I let Xavier in and shut and locked the door again.he was sitting on the bench in the window, I went and sat next to him. I pulled my knees to my chest and looked up at him. He stared at me looking almost worried.

" You know, I didn't know that she knew you, right?" He asked."I know." I replied."Good." He said sounding relieved. "Are you okay?""Yah, I'm okay. I just wish she would've told me." I said sadly.

He pulled me into his arms and ran his hand through my hair in a comforting manner. I put my head on his shoulder and closed my eyes. We sat like this for a while before he broke the silence.

"You need to feed." He said.I shook my head, not wanting to do it."Yes, please your still weak and I don't want to worry about losing you again." "Okay."

He brought his wrist up to my mouth. I took it in my hand and bit down. I let the liquid trickle down my throat until he started to pull back and I released his wrist. I looked up at him while licking the blood off of my lips. He stared at me. I started to think I still had something one my face.

"Is there something on my face?" I asked.He chuckled and said, "No, I just like looking at you."I smiled up at him and said, "I like looking at you too."

He leaned down and kissed my lips. It wasn't a passionate kiss but a sweet and sincere one. I started to yawn and feel sleepy. Xavier noticed.

"It's okay love, you can go to bed I will see you tomorrow." He said. He kissed me on the forehead and walked to the door. "Goodnight Gidget." And he left.

I took a shower and brushed my teeth. I put on grey shorts and a black AC/DC T-shirt, braided my hair and went to bed. I fell asleep minutes later.

I woke up and checked the clock, 11:30am. I got up and got ready, I got dressed(outfit at the top). I left my hair in its natural waves. I put on mascara and lipgloss and went downstairs. I'm going to talk to Liza today. I walked into the kitchen, then I saw Liza's short blonde hair. In an instant she turned and her blue eyes met my brown ones.

"Gidget I'm so sorry, I didn't mean for you to find out about me like that. I promise, just let me explain. I know you won't forgive me right away but you will forgive me at some point right?" She nervously rambled while chewing on her nails."Yes, I will forgive you but it's going to take time.""I understand.""I'll let you explain too."

Xavier was close I could feel him. He seemed worried. A moment later I felt an arm around me. Sparks scattered my skin letting me know it's Xavier. I turned in his arms and hugged him. I turned back to Liza waiting for her explanation.

"When I first met you it was because Winter needed someone to protect you when you were at school. So she called me I was supposed to act lost on my first day at a new school. Then you would help me and I would start working on being your friend. I was only supposed to be your friend till graduation but I couldn't just ditch you. Somewhere along the line you became my real friend. I know I lied about a lot and you probably don't feel like you know me but you do. You're still my best friend. My favorite color is green but my favorite food is O-. I don't go to see my grandma I go to visit my mate who he has in jail right now." She explained

"Why is he in jail?" I asked."He killed a lot of his own people including my parents. He worked with Victor who planned on taking over the throne, he committed high treason." Xavier said."He didn't do it because he wanted to Victor threatened him. He said if he didn't do as he said that he would kill his little sister." Liza said."I don't care what he told you he's just using you to get to me." He stated."Whose Victor?" I asked.

Liza turned to me and covered her mouth. Her eyes were wide like she said something she wasn't supposed to.

"Hopefully you'll never have to find out. He's just a horrible person." He said.I nodded, acknowledging his statement. I got a water and a banana chocolate chip muffin from the counter and walk into the living room. Xavier followed behind me. He sat down beside me on the couch as I ate and watched tv.

"Do you think you can ever trust Liza again?""Yes, but I think it's going to take some time.""That's understandable, considering you just found out that she's been lying to you your whole friendship about who she really is." He said.

"Yah, it just seems like everyone in my life lies to me.""I know." He said "Stephen & Landon are coming over today would it make you feel better if we all did something together?"I smiled, "Yah but make sure to invite Liza I don't want her to be left out.""Okay, I will."

"Can we play board games?" I asked excitedly.He chuckled and replied, "Would that make you happy?"I nodded my head eagerly."Then yes we can play board games." He replied and kissed my forehead."Landon and Stephen will be here in an hour." He said looking at his phone."Okay." I replied.

I must have fallen asleep, I woke up on the couch with a pillow under my head. I heard talking in the kitchen, so I walked in there. Landon, Stephen and Xavier were in there.

"Why haven't you marked her yet? Most mates it's done within a week." Landon said."I know but I don't want to rush things she's just now getting healthy again, I don't want to push it." Xavier said.I walked over to them ."Well if it isn't sleeping beauty." Stephen said."Hey guys." I said.I looked up at Xavier and said, "board games?"He nodded his head and smiled."Go get Liza then." I said.

He left to get her. I asked Stephen where the board games were and he went to get some. I heard something in the other room and I went to go check on it. I felt a pain in my chest as I went to Xavier's office. My eyes widen and tears slipped from my eyes. Xavier was in his office chair and Bianca was sitting on his lap kissing him, and he was kissing her back. I couldn't bare the sight anymore I turned and ran out the door. I ran until I couldn't run anymore. Was in the middle of the woods. I fell to my knees on the forest floor and sobbed. I thought we had something. That must be why he didn't want to mark me, he still likes Bianca. He shouldn't have lead me on. I thought I could trust him but I can't trust anyone but myself I just had to learn it the hard way. I cried until I finally fell asleep from exhaustion.

~~~

A/N

I feel like this chapter was kinda boring hopefully the ending helped make it less boring. Let me know what you thought.vote, comment & shareI hope you like the story so far.

~ Sadie

11423 words
~~~

Chapter 7

X avier's POV:

Before the kiss

I walked away from everyone to go get my sister. Damn it, I forgot to get Landon that contract he needs to sign. I walk to my office. I go and sit in my chair and go through my drawers. Found it, I noticed someone standing in my doorway. I recognize the red hair instantly.

"Bianca." I say emotionless. "Xavier." She replies in a fake sweet voice.

She walked up to me sitting on my desk. She needs to leave before Gidget sees her.

"What do you want?" I asked."I just want one thing then I'll leave, promi se.""And what's that?""This"

I was confused until her lips met mine. I automatically kissed her back. I don't know how long the kiss lasted. I pulled away think of Gidget. I pushed her away. Suddenly I was overwhelmed with sadness. I wasn't sad so that only meant one thing. Shit, she saw. No, I ran after her but she was already gone I couldn't see her anywhere. I can't sense her. I panicked. Why can't I sense her. I ran back inside.

"Landon! Stephen!" I yelled."What?" They both said looking worried."S he...she's gone, she saw but I didn't... I pushed her away."

I rambled panicking and running my hands through my hair. Stephen walked up to me and put his hands on my shoulders."Who? Whose gone?" Stephen asked."Gidget." I said as I sat on the couch and put my head in my hands."Why? What did she see?""Bianca kissed me and... I ... I kissed her back." His face went from worried to angry. "But I pushed her away the second I realized what I was doing I swear." I said in a rush."You still shouldn't have kissed her back." Landon said."I know""She's in danger now and it's all because of a misunderstanding." Landon said."Yes, it's all my fault and we have to get everyone to search for her Victor can't find out.""What if he already knows?" Stephen muttered to himself."We can't think like that... I can't lose her. I just got her." I said"Okay I'll go get everyone to search all around the house and woods."

I walk from the living room to my bedroom. I start to pace the room. It's all my fault. I shouldn't have let her get that close. I should have kicked her out from the beginning. I can't believe I kissed her back. If she gets hurt... or worse, no! I can't think about that. I'm barely keeping it together now.

6 hours later

Everyone was walking in the door. I walked up to them eagerly looking for her.

"Anything?" I asked. All of them shook their heads."THEN KEEP LOOKING!" I roared.They left the room in a hurry.I walked from behind my desk to the door."Where is she?" I yelled, punching a hole in the door.

4 hours later

I can't sleep I just keep thinking what if he has her. What if she's dead... no! I mean I'd feel that right? I can't sense her anymore though. I can't stop thinking about her I just want her to be safe. I don't care if she never wants to see my again just as long as I know she's alive and safe. Stephen walks into my room.

"X you need to sleep." He said."I can't sleep while I know she out there. She thinks I cheated. She's scared and hurt and it's all my fault." A stray tear rolls down my cheek. "I think I love her.""I know." Stephen said calmly."What?" I looked at him, surprised.

"I said, I know. I mean come on, you can't sleep, eat or even think straight because you think she might be in danger. You've never dated a girl for more than a week let alone lose sleep over one." He said."I love her and she doesn't even know it." I said."Get some sleep Xavier, you're no help if you can't even form a proper thought.""Okay, I'll try." I said in defeat.

Gidget's POV:

Morning after the kiss

I woke up laying on the forest floor under a tree. I took me a second before I remembered what happened. I looked down at my tattered and torn dress. Oh well, I got up and started walking, I need to find a road or something.

I walked for what felt like hours before I finally found a road. There were no cars. I started walking on the road. Maybe I'll see a car further down or a gas station. As I kept walking I couldn't shake the fear that someone was following me. I looked behind me but no one was there. I walked into something hard. I went to see what it was but something covered my mouth and nose and everything went dark.

I woke up in a concrete cell. It was dark but I could see what was definitely blood covering the wall in front of me. I went to move but was stopped. I looked down. I was chained to the floor, the chains looked like they were made of silver. Every time I move my skin burns. I guess silver + vampire = pain. I look frantically around the room. There's no way out that I can see. I pull on the chains panicking now. I pulled so much my wrists started to bleed.

The cell door started to open. I cowered in the corner afraid of what's on the other side. A older man with brown hair and eyes walked into the room. He had a chair in his hand. He brought it in front of me and sat down starring at me.

"You look like her. Except the eyes that's all me." He said, "How did Seraphina keep you a secret? How come I couldn't sense you before?""I don't know. I don't even know you. How did you know my mother?""You mean you don't know."I shook my head.

"Well let me explain then. You see your mother was my mate. When she was pregnant with you she left me. I guess she thought you would be safer without me. I couldn't find her anywhere after she left. It took me 4 years to find her again. Which leads me back to why didn't I know about you?" He said"Winter." I said.

"The witch? Your mother's friend?""Yes.""Ah, she made you human."I nodded my head."If you're my mothers mate does that mean you're my ...""Go on dear say it."

"Father."

"Ah, there it is. Took you long enough, really you must have your mother's brains. A little slow at best darling.""What do you want from me?""Oh well that's easy. You see you're Xavier's mate. I want to take down Xavier and in order to do that I need to take down you first.""But I'm your daughter." I pleaded."So." He said coldly.

~~~
~~~

A/NI dropped a couple hints in this chapter. Let me know what you think is going to happen next. I hope you enjoyed the story so far.

~ Sadie

1207 words

Chapter 8

• •

Xavier's POV:

A day later

The search party came back to my office. I stood from my seat to greet them.

"Anything?" I said hopefully.One of the men walked to me holding something. "This is all we found, sir." He said handing me the piece of cloth.I brought it up to my nose. I smells like her."She couldn't have gotten that far. The only way that would be possible is if someone helped her." He said, "Or took her."

That's what I was afraid of. "We need to find out if Victor has her."Stephen walks into the room holding a small box in his hands. He looks up at me, his eyes are filled with sorrow. He hands me the box and says, "He has her."

I look into the box that confirms all my worst nightmares are coming true. A tear falls from my eyes as I see a piece of brown hair with clumps of blood in it. Under the hair was a photograph of Gidget, she's chained to the floor with silver chains. Her wrist are bleeding, her dress is hardly there it's all ripped and covered in blood. She lashing on the floor looking half dead. I can't look at it anymore. There's a note on the top of the box.

You know what I want Xavier. Give it to me and get the girl. If not more pieces of her will be on there way. I'm thinking fingers next but maybe just skin. I can't decide. I might just do both. It's your choice Xavier.

~ V

Gidget's POV:

where the last chapter ended

He stalked towards me as I backed into the corner as far as the chains would let me.

"Tsk tsk, now you know you can't run away silly child" he said as he grabbed my hair and rammed my head into the concrete wall.

I felt blood dripping down my face as black spots quickly appeared. I hunched over on the floor in hope of not getting hurt more. It didn't work he started to kick me in the stomach repeatedly. Tears fell from eyes. He laughed and punched me in the face that was when everything finally went black.

When I woke up I couldn't move. Just breathing hurts. I coughed and looked at me hand. It was covered in blood. That can't be good. I heard the door open and I scrambled into the corner no matter how much it hurt I was too afraid to care.

"Hello daughter." He said. "Xavier is taking too long to reply, so I'm decided to have a little fun. You my dear are the only person here to play with. I killed all the others." He whispered the last part putting his finger to his mouth in a shh sign.

He walked to me. I flinched as he took my wrist and unlocked the chain. He did the same with the other but quickly put a silver chain around my neck and started to walk to the door pulling me along.

"Come on I don't have all day." He said sternly.I followed him as he walked down a long hall then went to the double doors on the right. There was a almost cross like silver structure with cuffs standing in the middle of the room. On the walls there was all kinds of weapons, knives and many other things. He pulled me to the cross like thing and pushed me against it. I tried to fight him but between the beating, silver and lack of blood I was no match. He put my wrists in the cuffs the whole front of my body burned from the silver pressed against it.

"I'll be right back I just want to get someone so he can join in on the fun." He said.

I could see him leave but I heard the door shut. I frantically looked around the room for anything to help or get me out but everything was on the walls. I heard the door open and close again.

"Son I need you to give her 100 lashes. Got it." He ordered.

Wait son, I have a brother. But he's going to hurt me too. Does he know?

"Father, May I ask why she gets so many lashes.""She Just is now carry on."

I heard some shuffling and then I felt it. A sharp pain all across my back. I felt as though the end had a silver blade in it. I felt my skin brake and blood flow down my back. After three lashes I was crying.

"Please, please stop I'm your sister. Why are you doing this?" I begged

He stopped I breathed a sigh of relief. "My sister?" He asked."Yah so she's my daughter, now can we continue?""No! I won't hurt my sister.""Fine then you can watch, and Alexander don't think your off the hook. You will watch and now she will get more lashes."

The whip hit my back once more this time with ten times the force. I sobbed.

"No!" Alex screamed."Stay there or she dies."

He started the lashes once more. By ten my whole back was numb. I was slouched onto the cross which was burning my skin. I could see the black spots forming, I felt another hit and everything went black.

I woke up when I heard the door close loudly. Someone opened my cuffs and I crumbled to the floor but the caught me.

"Why would he do this to you?" Alex said."Xavier." I coughed."What about Xavier"M..mate." I struggled to say."Don't worry I'll get you out of here somehow." He said in comforting voice.

After that I blacked out again. I woke up to someone carrying me. It felt like they were running. I looked around but it was too dark to see much, all I could make out was trees. I looked to see who was carrying me. It was Alex.

"What's going on?" I asked."I'm getting you out of here." He said."Xavier is at the end of the woods if we can make it there we're good."

If? I don't like the sound of that. I could almost see the line at the end of the woods. We got closer and then I saw him.Xavier.

~~~
~~~

Chapter 9

I heard a stick break behind us. I turned to look not caring how much pain I was in. I could see the shadow of someone chasing us.

"Someone is right behind you." I whispered to Alex."I know." He said.

The shadow keeps getting closer.

"It's Victor."Alex nods.

There's more people behind him. I begin to panic. Victor close enough to fully see now and he's steadily gain on us. My heart races faster. I can't go back, I won't survive much longer there.

"GET THEM!" Victor orders his men.

He lunges at us, tackling Alex. The force at the speed we were going launched onto the ground. I rolled until I hit a tree trunk. I cringed at the feeling of my back hitting the tree when it was recently hurt anyway. Pain shot through my whole body. I couldn't move. I can't feel my limbs. I started to feel really dizzy.

"GIDGET!" I could hear Xavier yell.

I tried to speak but nothing came out. Tears started to flow down my cheeks. I could see Victor punching Alex repeatedly and I couldn't do anything. I heard someone step near me I instantly panic in fear of being hurt even more.

"Gidget, it's me, it's okay." Xavier said lifting my head onto his lap.

No matter how mad I am at him or how much I wanted to be away from him when I left right now I'm relieved he's here. Xavier looked like he was going to burst into tears as he looked down at me.

"Can you move?" He asked quietly.

I shook my head a little just enough he could tell what I meant.

I looked back at Alex Victor was going to kill him, he had him by his throat. I kept trying to yell for him, get someone to help. Nothing came out and I'm starting to get too weak to try. Xavier could tell I was about to pass out.

"No...no..no, stay with me please." He begged. I looked back to Alex, "Help Alex.......brother." It was so quiet I don't think he heard it. My eyes began drooping and I gave into the darkness.

Xavier's POV:

I held Gidget's almost lifeless body in my arms. I thought back to what she said. I looked around for Alex he was the one who contacted me. I found him being pinned to a tree be Victor who was hold him by the neck. I signaled for Stephen to come to me.

"Take her home and calls the doctors, there's some of my blood in the fridge she needs it right away." I said. Stephen picked her up and said, "I'll take care of her." I nodded. Once I could see she was safe I charged for Victor. I yanked him from Alex and onto the ground. I started to punch him repeatedly. He started to laugh.

"Why are you laughing?" I demanded."Kill me." He said."Oh, you think I'm going to kill you right now. Not a chance I'm going to take you somewhere you can't get out of, somewhere I'm going to bring you to the brink of death so many times you'll be begging me to kill." I told him.

His smile dropped as I delivered one last punch that knocked him out. I picked him up by the collar and drug him. I looked back at Alex who was just standing there.

"Coming?" I asked."Me?" He said completely astonished."You saved her and you're her brother, so your always welcome. Come on." I said.

He started to follow, when we got to the car I popped the trunk and threw Victor in and shut it. I drove back to the house and I started to panic about if Gidget was okay or not. It was dark but I could see the outline of bruises, her dress was barley there it was all torn an tattered. I could see blood in all different spots, when Stephen took her from my arms they were completely covered in blood. What did he do to her.

I stormed into the house and asked Stephen where she was. He said he bedroom so I went there immediately. She was laying there still unconscious. There were three doctors around her doing different things.

"Is she going to be okay?" I asked worriedly.

"She should be alright she has lost a lot of blood and hasn't feed in days. The little bit that was given to her help but she needs more to heal. I recommend you staying with her. You being her mate should help her heal faster. Give her some of your blood. The silver burns on her wrist and front half shouldn't scare, as for the lashes on her back it looks as though she was whipped and a blade of silver at the end. Her back will most likely scare because of the severity of the wounds." He explained. I tried to absorb the information. "We'll leave you two alone." He said as they walked out of the room.

I look at her battered body and a tear fell from my eye. I could have lost her. I almost did. I sat on the bed beside her. I bit my wrist and put it to her mouth. She didn't react I started to worry but then one of her hands reached to hold me there. I breathed a sigh of relief. Then her beautiful brown orbs opened and looked into mine.

Gidget's POV:

I opened my eyes and was met with brilliantly blue ones. I pulled my mouth from his wrist remember what had happened I looked down at my hands not wanting to look at him anymore.

"I know what you thought you saw." He said."Thought." I scoffed."Yes, thought. I wasn't cheating if you had stayed longer you would have seen he push her off.""You kissed her back." I whispered.

"I know, I shouldn't have but I stopped once I realized what I was doing. I know you won't take my word of it and I don't blame you. That's why I want to do a memory search with you again I have some things I want to show you anyway.""Okay." I agreed.

~~~

A/N

Sorry it's a short chapter but I wanted to save the memory search for chapter 10. I hope you enjoyed the chapter.Please, like, vote & comment.

~ Sadie

1081 words
~~~

Chapter 10

Xavier put his wrist in front of my mouth. He took my wrist and looked to me as if asking permission. I nodded my head and we both bit down at the same time. I let the sweet liquid trickle down my throat till I felt him pull away and I did the same. He took my arm and made a small cut, then doing the same to his. He looked at me with those blue eyes and pressed our arms together.

I looked around we were in the house still but we were in Xavier's office. Why are we here? I looked around for him. I saw a young boy, he looked like he was between 9 or 11 years old. I went to touch his shoulder but I went through. He looked around the room when his eyes met mine I knew instantly. I'd know those blue eyes anywhere. This must be what Xavier want to show me other than the kiss. I sat on the floor in the corner of the room since I can't do anything but watch.

"Dad!" Little Xavier yelled. "Mom!"

A pretty woman rushed into the room. She grabbed Xavier and ran to the end of the room where there was a fireplace. She turned Xavier to face her he had tears in his eyes.

"Xavier, you have to go to the safe room and stay there no matter what. Do you understand?" He nodded his head. She leaned down to kiss his forehead. "Remember me and your father love you no matter what happens."

There was a loud crash behind them. Her eyes instantly panicked.

"Go! Xavier you have to go now!" He started into the fireplace but looked back. "Go!"

He went in all the way. I didn't move but suddenly I was in the room with Xavier. It was a plain concrete room with a bed and shelves of survival equipment. Canned foods, blankets, water and more. He went to the bed, pulled his knees to his chest and sobbed quietly. I wanted nothing more than to comfort him but I knew I couldn't. Suddenly there was yelling outside of the room.

"Mom!" He yelled and ran to the door and back into the fireplace. He stopped at what he saw. I gasped with tears forming in my eyes. Victor had Xavier's mom, with a knife to her throat. There was a man standing on the other side of the desk. I guess that's Xavier's dad. They look a lot alike.

"Give me the thrown." Victor sneered. "Or she dies.""Don't!" She yelled.

Victor pulled her closer with the knife digging into her neck enough to draw blood.

"I can't." Xavier's father said in a sad voice."Fine, then you give me no choice.""You always had a choice Victor, you just choose wrongly and that's why you will never be on the thrown."

Victor rammed her head on the desk, then turned her to face him and look into his eyes. He then stabbed her in the stomach. He didn't stop with that he kept stabbing. It all seemed to much like when my mother was killed. Memories rushed back but I quickly snapped out of it when Xavier's father yelled.

"NO!" He yelled in anguish.

Three of Victor's men rushed in as he charged Victor. Two held his arms back and kicked the back of his knees to make him kneel. He looked down tears falling from his eyes. The third man walked behind him and broke his neck. His limp body fell to the floor. Xavier started to run to his parents but before he could Winter appeared out of nowhere and pulled him back taking him to the safe room again. She held him tightly as he sobbed for his parents.

"H...he k..killed them." He cried. "Their gone.""I know." She said. "But you have to be strong, your people need you right now no one knows you even exist. Your uncles are on their way. They will take the thrown until your ready."

"I don't want it!" He said angrily."I know but it's what you need to do. Sometimes you have to do what's best for others.""Now lets get you out of here I think you've had enough sadness for a lifetime." Winter said.

Everything went black and we were taken to Xavier's office again. This time is recent though. Xavier walked into the office sitting in his chair and looking for something. Then Bianca showed up in the doorway.

"Bianca." He said."Xavier." She said in a sickly sweet voice.

She walked over to his desk. It took everything in me to keep watching knowing what was about to happen.

"What do you want?""I just want one thing then I'll leave, promise.""And what is that?" She walked closer to him and said, "This."

She leaned over him and pressed her lips to his. He kissed her back. Tears started to fall all over again. Then his face changed to regret and sadness. He pushed her away. That was when I saw them and ran out of the house. He instantly got up and ran for me not caring about Bianca at all. He was telling the truth. He still kissed her back though and it's going to take time for me to trust him again.

Suddenly we were back to reality. Looked to Xavier he got up and started pacing the room. Running his fingers through his hair he began to talk.

"I'm sorry, so sorry... I know you may never forgive me I just wanted you to know the truth. And I understand if you want to reject me I'll tell you how just as long as you're safe and happy. I'll do anything." He was rambling.

I got up from the bed to stop his pacing. I hadn't even thought about how I'm still hurt and weak. When I tried to stand I instantly started to fall. Xavier caught me looking at me with worried eyes. He picked me up and sat me on the bed I winced as I leaned back.

"Are you okay? You can't do that you need to rest and heal. You're still too weak."

I put my fingers up to his mouth to shut him up. He looked at me surprised. I hugged his torso, even if I was still upset with him right now I just wanted him to hold me.

"W...what are you doing?""Hugging, ever heard of it?"

He laugh lightly and pulled back a little.

"No, just hold me." I said softly. "Please."

He nodded his head and laid beside me. I put my head on his chest. Calmness washed over me as I fell asleep moments later.

~~~

A/N

A lot happened in this chapter, I hope you enjoyed it.Please share, vote and comment.
~~~

~ Sadie

Chapter 11

1 week later

I've finally healed and I'm back to normal. However I do have scars from the whip. They litter my back and some of my arms. I feel very self conscious about them. I've been wearing clothes so that no one sees them. Today I went with a outfit that covers them too. (outfit at the top).

I haven't seen Xavier for the past two days. He's been in the basement with Victor. I don't even want to know what's going on down there. That's a lie I kinda do but I know if I go down there that I will regret it later. I wish he would come up from there. I feel like he's avoiding me.

I wanted to tell him how I feel about him and that I want to give him another chance but every time I look for him he's no where to be found. Its getting frustrating.

I go downstairs to once again look for Xavier. I go to his office and knock on the door but no answer. I turn to leave and go to the kitchen I heard a crash.I turn back abruptly and open the door only to find a broken vase in the corner of the room. Xavier is behind his desk with his head in his hands. I can see splattered blood on the ends of his dress shirt and across the middle. I walk to him and place my hand on his shoulder. His head jerks up and his glossy blue eyes met my brown ones.

"Xavier." I say softly.

I see a tear fall from his right eye as he pulls me to him. His arms snake around my waist and he lays his head on my chest. I was surprised for a second but quickly put my hands to his hair and run my fingers through his hair.

"What happened?" I ask.

"I don't understand." He says more to himself than me.

"Understand What?"

"How he could do it. He had no reason he just wanted power and he was willing to kill innocent people and make a boy an orphan for his foolish wants. How can one person be so heartless?" He said.

"Some people are just cruel and heartless. Some have reasons. Some it's almost like they were born that way. I don't know how anyone could do such things and yet people seem to." I said.

He pulled back from me and looked down at his desk and said,

"Sorry. I don't know what came over me I just needed to hold you."

"It's fine. Xavier I need to tell you something."

"I understand if you wish to reject me I'll accept it if it will make you happy."

"No, I"

"It's okay really, just go."

"Xavier will you please shut up and let me speak!" I say loudly.

He looks to me surprised but nodded his head.

"Good, now as I was saying. I've had a lot of time to think about us this past week and I want to give us a another chance. However my trust doesn't run far for good reason this is a one time offer, no more chances. I believe that you have feelings for me and I understand if you don't feel the same but Xavier I think I love you and it's fine that you don't," my babbling was cut short when I was suddenly pulled into a kiss.

As our lips molded together sparks spread across my whole body. I raised my arms and my fingers gripped the back of his head trying to pull him impossibly closer.his arm tight around my waist and one hand in my hair. The kiss lasted for what seemed like forever and a short time all at once until he pulled away from me. Resting his head against mine.

"I love you too." He breathed.

"What?" I asked surprised.

He smirked and said, "I love you."

A grin spread across my face. "You do?"

He nodded full on smiling now.

He leaned down and gave me lips a quick peck.

He looked to me slightly worried. "How long has it been since you fed."

My smile dropped and I looked down. "I don't know a few days......a week."

"Gidget, this is why I put some of my blood in the fridge for you, you have to remember to eat I can't lose you. I already almost did. I just got you back." He said

"I'm sorry, it's just I forget and I kept thinking about you and I couldn't find you."

"It's okay, but you need to eat."

He put his wrist up to my mouth. "Come on. Drink."

"But if you already have some in the fridge then I don't have to bite you."

"It's better for you if it's straight from the source so drink up."

"Okay."

I lowered my lips to his wrist and bit down letting the blood coat my throat. I felt all my senses heighten I didn't know how weak I felt until then. After awhile he pulled back and I released his wrist. I looked up at him and licked my lips tasting the last of his blood.

"Don't do that." He said.

"Do what?" I said innocently while licking my lips again.

He growled and pulled me in for another heated kiss. I pulled back looking up into his eyes as he smiled. I smiled back and laid my head on his chest. Then I thought of the blood on his shirt.

"Xavier?"

"Hmm?"

"Why is there so much blood on your shirt?"

He stiffened at the question. "Well, I was interrogating Victor and I may have got carried away. He won't be hurting anyone again."

"Good." I whispered.

"What?" He said completely flabbergasted.

"I said good." I said a little louder.

He nodded his head. I pulled away from him and went to the door.

"Where are you going?" He said panicked.

"I want to go to the garden. Coming?" I asked holding my hand out for him.

He nodded and took my hand as we went to the garden. I have a good feeling about us this time I think it might work.

~~~

A/N

I hope you like the chapter, sorry it's been so long since I updated.Next chapter will have Xavier's POV and what happened to Victor.Vote, comment & share.Please.

~ Sadie
~~~

Chapter 12

A /NSorry it took so long. Enjoy .~ Sadie

Xavier's POV:

After they captured Victor

I stayed with Gidget until I knew she would make it through. Then I made my way to the basement where Victor was being kept.I walked to his concrete cell which is similar to the one he kept Gidget in judging by the photo he sent me.I see him sitting in the far left corner.I slam the door shut make his head look up at me as a sinister smile spread across his face.

"Well, well, well, the great Xavier finally decided to give me a visit, to what do I owe the honor." Victor said.

"I'm in no mood for your game Victor." I sneered while glaring at him." Why did you do it?" I asked.

"Do what?" "You hurt her.""Are you really that stupid? She's your weakness and I want the crown.""She's your daughter.""So.""Have you ever cared about anyone but yourself? Are you really so heartless?""I tried the caring thing once, it didn't last long."

"Wanting the crown isn't the only reason you hurt her. You knew you would get what you wanted from me with that picture you sent but you continued to hurt her after. Why?"

He looked down at the floor before he started to laugh.

"She just looked so much like her.""Who?""Sera.""Her mother? Why do you want to hurt her mother?"He laughed again. "Oh, pore Xavier your so far behind.""She was your mate, why hurt her."

He started laughing in a sinister way again, I can't understand what's so funny.I walked over to him and pulled his hair back to make him look into my eyes.

"Tell me!" I roared."Xavier all the answers are right in front of you all you have to do is connect the dots."

I dropped his head and thought back to what I know so far. He noticed my thoughtful look.

"Here let me help some,"

1. Gidget is my daughter 2. Sera was my mate3. Sera was killed4. Gidget was kept as a secret5. Alex is Gidget's older brother 6. Gidget can only drink vampire blood

"Does that help any." Victor said.

"How do you know she can't drink human blood.""Haven't you wondered why she can't drink human blood."I gave him a curious look.

"Since obviously you're not going to figure it out on your own let me tell you a story."

I don't understand why he's not putting up any fight on telling the truth.

"I tried to love my mate like you're supposed to but about a year into it I started cheating, hence how Alex came about. After Alex it confirmed my infidelity to Sera. She would threaten to leave and I would take my anger out on her. I wanted an heir and Alex was that. Sera just couldn't give me that and it angered me.

I wanted the crown and I planed on getting it. I had already failedonce but I wouldn't let that happen again, in order for me to win I needSomething no one else had, the ultimate weapon.

I order to do that I need something expendable, something that if it worked I could easily control but if it went south nothing important would be lost.So of course I went with the most logical answer and chose my mate.I started giving her my blood instead of human little by little until all she had was Vampire blood. Little did I know she wasn't the weapon I was creating but my child was. One night when I came home she was no where to be found.I looked for her for 4 years before I finally found her.

She had the help of her little witch friend to protect her but she made onemistake. She went back home to see her dying mother. I knew she would and that's why I had one of my guards posted outside. He followed her home and reported back to me.

I went to her house and we yelled at one another, I could tell she was frightened and I liked it. I was in such a rage I just stabbed her and once I started I couldn't stop.I just kept stabbing. Then I just left and told my guards to clean up the mess. I had no idea about Gidget until that one day when I could sense her .I sent my guards to get her instantly.

I didn't plan on hurting her at first until I found out she was on your land.Then I have one of my men to investigate and they found out she wasyour mate and I had the perfect opportunity. So I took it. When I saw her she looked so much like sera and may have taken it a little to far."

There was so much information. He mother was killed just like my parents because of Victor. Flashes of the night my parents died kept Running throughout my head. He did all that to her. He hurt her more than anyone else ever could not only physically but emotionally. I filled with rage I was practically shaking. I could here uncontrollable laughter. He was laughing.

"How could you!" I yelled as he kept laughing.

I pulled his hair back and rammed his head against the wall. I kept doing it o couldn't stope he needed to pay for what he did. I kicked him in the stomach. I grabbed the baseball bat from the wall it had barb wire wrapped around the end. I just kept hitting him. I couldn't stop. I kept going until he was unrecognizable.I had blood all over me.

I rush out of the room and told the guards to clean it up.I went to my office and started pacing the floor. I can't believe I did that.he need to suffer. I let him off to easy. Then I thought of Gidget she has no idea. I have to tell her but it's going to break her even more. I started throwing things in the office not caring what I break.I'll tell her when she's better and only if she wants to know.

A/N

I'm sorry it's been so long. I hope the chapter was to your liking.All is revealed but how is Gidget going to react.Let me know your thoughts in the comments. I love any kind of feedback.

VOTE, COMMENT, & SHARE

~ Sadie

Chapter 13

----

2 weeks later

Gidget's POV:

I'm completely healed now. Xavier and I have been doing really well. I think we're finally back to How thing we're before everything got messed up.He seems like something is on his mind though. He's still distant even though I know he's trying not to be. He's not telling me something. Our bond is back and stronger than ever. I can sense him yet again and for some reason that gives me sense of security.

I still have scars but they aren't as bad as they were. The only ones that are really noticeable are on my back. I've been hiding them from Xavier still. They are ugly and I don't want him to see them. The back of my shirt had a cut out part but that's why I wore a sweater with it.(outfit at the top.) I walk downstairs and don't see Xavier anywhere but I can sense him so he must be in his office. As I walk through the doorway I see Xavier there, his hands in his hair and looking down at the desk. I don't what it is that's stressing him out so much but he needs to get it off his chest.

"Xavier?" I say quietly as I approach his desk.

He looks up at me and instantly his eyes brighten a little but there's still sadness and worry hidden behind them.

"Gidget." He replies softly.

I walk around the desk to him. He stands and embraces me lovingly.

"You need to tell me whatever it is I'll understand."

He pulls back with a surprised look on his face that's then masked with sadness.

"I know I just don't want to hurt you any more than I already have." He says.

I place my hand on his cheek and look into the mesmerizing blue eyes and say, "It's okay. Tell me."

He searches my eyes for any doubt but I show none know if I did he would back out.

"You don't know everything about who Victor was, him and your mother were mates. For a while they were happy and Victor was a good mate. About a year after they were wed and mated he started to abuse her. What started out as only in moments of anger turned to an everyday occurrence. If she hadn't of been a vampire she never would have survived such cruelty. When your mother found out she was pregnant she knew she had to leave. She couldn't let him hurt you like he hurt her." He said.

I suddenly feel weak so I sit on the desk.

"Seraphina's best friend in high school was Winter who was a witch. She knew she was the only person who could help her get out but she had to wait for the right moment. What she didn't know is that Victor had been slowly giving her his blood the whole time she was pregnant. Which explains why you can only drink vampire blood. When she went for Winter, Winter could only use a protection spell but it was weak if Victor got too close he could sense you both. So winter went to some elder witches and did some research and she found the spell that made you both appear human and only have human qualities. She cast the spell when you were born but the spell was only temporary and would wear off completely on you 19 birthday." He continued and I felt like my whole world had been flipped upside down.

"When you were four and your mother was murdered it was because Victor had found her. Victors the one who killed your mother." He said not daring to look me in the eyes.

"How do you know all this?" I asked as I felt hot tears streaming down my face.

"Victor told me before I killed him and I confirmed by getting the rest of the story from Winter. I didn't want to tell you until I had the whole truth." He stated.

I start to head for the door but a hand around my wrist stops me in my tracks.

"Gidget please, don't push me away." He pleads. "I love you."

I look up at him. "I love you too, I just... I need a little time to process things." I say.

He nods understandingly and release my wrist from his tight grip.

I go back to my room and pull off my sweater, feeling hot from all the crying. I feel tired so I lay down thinking I'll take a sort nap.Shortly after my hated hits the pillow the darkness takes over.

After Gidget left Xavier's office.

Xavier's POV:

I keep pacing the room and reviewing what just happened in head. I know I had to tell her but I can't help but feeling as though I caused her pain. I can feel it through the bond. Such sadness, confusion and anger. It's my fault she was doing better, I should have left it alone.

NO! I can't think like that she had to know. It was destroying me to keep such a thing from her. If I hadn't told her it would have ruined our relationship and the trust that we have just recently built back up. I just I can't lose her again I don't know what I do if she was hurt again or worse.

I want so badly to just go and comfort her but I know she needs to be alone right now. Her whole worldWas just crushed and that's going to take time. No matter what she needs I'm going to be there for her I'm never making my past mistakes again. She won't be alone not while I'm alive.

~~~

A/N

I know it's been a while and I'm sorry. I also know it's a pretty short chapter. I do however hope that you enjoyed it. I'm sorry it's been so long I just haven't had any motivation to write lately and don't want to write when I don't want to. I want to give you guys the best possible story I can even if that means taking a little longer to post chapters sometimes. However I do feel as though this story is coming to an end. Which could possibly be why I've been avoiding writing I hate endings. Have a great day.

VOTE, COMMENT AND SHARE.

~ Sadie
~~~

Chapter 14

Xavier's POV:

Same night

I keep pacing the room worrying if Gidget is okay.I can't take it anymore I just need to see her and know she's okay.I walk up the stairs to her room. I hesitate to open the door but slowly turn the handle.I see Gidget sleeping on the bed. She starts to stir in her sleep and slowly awaken. When she does she gets up facing away from me.

The back of her shirt is open. I stared at her back for a moment not knowing how to react. Scars scattered across her skin showing the pain she with through because of her father. Fury started to course through my Bain's the longer I looked. I wish I made Victor suffer morehe deserved to suffer more.

I walk up behind he and gently touched he back. She flinched and sadness overcame me as I backed away from her. She turned quickly andlooked me in the eyes. I could see the worry as she rushed over too me.

"I'm sorry... I didn't mean too... I just... I" "Why didn't you tell me?" I interrupted her.

She looked down at her feet not willing to meet my eyes.

"Tell you what?" She said quietly."About the scars Gidget, you said you were fine and healed.""I... you were so angry already and ..." she mumbled something at the end I couldn't understand."What?""They're ugly and I didn't want you to see them."

I tilt her chin up so she can look into my eyes.

"Gidget, I love you and I always will no matter what you look like. Though your beautiful the scars only add to that because they show how strong you are. You've been though a lot and these show your story. Gidget you amazing you just need to be able to see it yourself."

I see a lonely tear stream down her face. I gently brush it away with my thumb as she leans into my hand. She turns her head and softly kisses my hand.

"Thank you." She says."No need to thank me for speaking the truth." I smile down as her.

She gets on her tiptoes and leans in to gently kiss my lips. She goes to pull away but I pull her back for another kiss and I hear her laugh.She pulls away only to pull me into a close embrace.

"I'd never made it through if it wasn't for you.""That's not true, you're stronger than you think."

For once everything seemed to just fit in place and I felt...

happy.

Gidget's POV:

2 weeks later

Finally everything between Xavier and I seemed to be going smoothly. I ever knew you could love one person so intensely. I feel like without him the day are a little darker but when he's near everything is suddenly clear again.It's amazing, simply exhilarating. We have such a strong bond at thins pointit's hard to imagine not being with him.

It was later in the evening and already getting dark outside. I walk into Xavier's office and see him sitting doing paperwork. I go up behind him and lay my hands on his shoulders. I instantly feel the tension leave him.He leans back and looks up at me with a smile. I lean down to give him a quick peck on the lips. He grabs my arm to pull me around the chair so I'm nowfacing him. I giggle as he pulls me onto his lap.his grin widens.

"What?" I say."Nothing, I just love that sound."

I shake my head as he pulls me close and I run my fingers through his hair.He leans in for another kiss and I kiss him back not wanting this Perfect moment to end. He picks me up and sets me back on my feet again.He gets up and turns to face me.

"I have a surprise for you." He said."What?""I just told you it's a surprise.""Turn around.""What? Why?""Well do you want to know the surprise or not."

I mumbled under my breath as I turned around. I felt something go over my eyes.He put a blindfold on me.

"It will be way to difficult to lead you out there I already know.""Well then how do you plan on.... what? Hey!"

I was cut off by him picking my up Lois Lane style.

"Put me down!""Not yet."

It seemed like we hadn't gone very far and he stopped. He sat me down and took his place standing behind me.

"Are you ready?" He asked.

I nodded my head excitedly.I could hear him lightly laugh at my reaction.I felt his hand behind me slowly untying the blindfold. As it finally stared to lower my vision was flooded with beautiful lights scattered across the lovely garden.In the center there sat a table with a candle Lit dinner set on it.

I turned around and jumped into his arms hugging him like my life depended on it.

"Thank you." I sincerely told him."Your welcome." He said kissing the top of my head.

Through the night we talked and laughed and everything Feldman just... well... perfect.Towards the end of He dinner Xavier seem nervous about something. I couldn't place what though. As I was About to ask he finally spoke up.

"Gidget I have something I need to tell you... well, ask you."

I timidly nod my head.

"Well you see I ...."

"I've wanted to ask for a while ...."

"Gidget,"

A/N

Sorry it's been so long yet again. I hope to get back into more of a routine soon. I hope you enjoyed the chapter. Please let me know any thought on the story I'm open to any kind of feedback.Any predictions for the next chapter?PLEASE VOTE, COMMENT AND SHARE!

~Sadie

Chapter 15

G idget's POV:

Same night

"Gidget, will you officially become my mate?""Officially?"

He took my hand in his and said, "There's a ceremony, like a wedding then there's the marking and the coronation for you to be queen because I am the king."

"Queen?" I whispered.

It all just seems so unreal. I mean me queen.

"But how can I be queen? I don't know anything about the vampires and they don't even know me." I said.

He pressed his hands against my face gently to make my eyes meet his.

"You're amazing and will be a great queen. The people will love you. You'll learn our ways, we have time they don't expect you to become the perfect queen overnight."

He stood up and I did the same. As we stood there he gazed into my eyes and leaned in to give me a loving kiss on the lips. Then he looked at me searching for any sign to the question he asked.

I looked up at him and nodded my head. "Yes." I said softly.

A big smile broke across his lips. He looked like a child on Christmas Day.

"Yes?" He asked.

I nodded still smiling.

"Yes!" He yelled as he picked me up and spun me around.

I couldn't help but laugh I have never been so happy.

"So... when will it be?"

"Next week?"

I looked at him with wide eyes.

"Too fast?"

I shook my head. " no, it's perfect." I said as I gave him a quick kiss.

We walked hand in hand back to the house. After we got back and went to his office he spoke up again.

"We need to get you a dress for the wedding."

"Okay..."

"Do you have a way of getting in touch with Liza?"

"Yes."

"Can you see if she would come and help me." I said looking down at my hands.

"Of course, I'm sure she'd love too." He said.

"So how exactly does this ceremony work?" I asked.

"Well it's almost the same as a human wedding just at the end we mark each other."

I look to him with wide eyes.

"Does it hurt?" I asked genuinely concerned.

He laughed at my panicked state and put his hand on my cheek.

"No it won't hurt, it only hurt if the other person isn't your mate."

"Okay." I nodded feeling slightly better now.

"Can I have the number to call Liza?" I asked.

"You don't need to call her she never left."

"What? But I haven't seen her."

"That's because she's only come out of her room for food and to visit her mate."

"Oh..."

I feel bad for the way I treated her. I should have gave her more of a chance.

"She's still in the same room."

"Okay, I'm going to see her."

He nodded as I went to the door.

I made my way up the stairs and to her room. I went to knock but my hand stopped before it hit the door. I'm not sure what I shouldsay to her. What if she doesn't forgive me? Ugh, you know what I'm juststressing myself out I'll never know if I don't try.

I take a deep breath and knock on the door. I hear nothing for awhile but then there was slight shuffling behind the door. The doorknob started to turn to reveal my best friend.

"Liza I'm so sorry, I shouldn't have acted like that, your my best friend and always will be.."

I was cut off by her putting her hand over my mouth and lightly laughing.

"Gidg it's okay. I know. I only kept my distance so you had time to adjust."

I smiled behind her hand and she moved it away.I jumped and gave her a bear hug like my life depended on it.She just laughed and hugged me back.

"Oh! I have something to ask you." I said.

"What?" She asked.

"Will you help me go dress shopping?"

"Of course but what's it for?"

I looked down at my hands but that was enough to give her the answer.

She started jumping up and down."Oh! You guys are FINALLY getting mated!"

I couldn't help but laugh at how excited she was and I nodded my head. She went to get her purseand practically drug me out of the house.

" I didn't mean right this second but okay." I said while still laughing.

We got in her car and headed to the store.

When we arrived at the store I noticed all the dresses were way out of my price range and Liza seemed to notice.

"Gidg it's fine X can pay for it. Trust me he'd hardly notice the money is gone."

I'm still a bit iffy about it. "I mean that's a lot though."

"Come on he's your mate and loves you it's fine just pick a dress."

I looked through all the choices in my size so many to choose from and all different colors. Oh no color!

"Does it have to be white like a wedding dress?" I asked.

"No, you can wear whatever color dress you want."

I smiled from ear to ear I know the dress I want then. I grabbed it and went to the dressing room to try it on.

When I came out Liza was standing there. "Oh that's definitely the dress Gidget it looks amazing."

I took the dress up and bought it on a credit card Xavier had given me but I hadn't used until now.I can't wait until he see's the dress.

Liza ran through the store like a madman because she saw the perfect dress that was similar in color to mine.I couldn't help but laugh at her. I love my best friend.

We take our dresses and shoes and head for home And I couldn't be more excited.

A/N

I'm so sorry it took so long for me to write this chapter. I hope you enjoyed it even tho it is short but don't worry more is to come.However there is only one chapter left but if anyone wants a book 2 I will happily write one.PLEASE, LIKE, COMMENT, VOTE & SHAREI love all you readers.Thank you for reading

~ Sadie

Chapter 16

F inal chapter

Ceremony day

Gidget's POV:

This week has been my happiest week yet. Me and Xavier are better than ever and I can't wait to spend the rest of my life with the man I love.Today is the big day. I keep having this off feeling but everyone keeps saying it's just nerves. I'm sure that's all. Today will be a day I never forget.

I have to get ready for everything so I start with my hair.

I finished with lots of help from Liza cause I'm not too great with hair. Now to the part I really need Liza for. My makeup.

She starts with my eye makeup and even does some winged eyeliner and false lashes.

Next was my lips which I wanted red cause if I'm gonna wear lipstick why not.

When she finished I looked in the mirror. I couldn't believe it was me.I love it. Liza's so good at hair and makeup which is good cause I'm not great with it.Now all that's left is my dress which I will put on when Liza gets done putting on her dress. A few moments later she walks out in He dress.

She looks great. Now I have to put on my dress.And then it's the beginning of the rest of my life with Xavier.I go to put on my dress and shoes. I can't believe it's happening but at the same time I wish it happened sooner.

I finally get the dress on and I'm all ready.

I'm ready so me and Liza go to the aisle which is outside because we agreed it fit us perfectly to have a garden wedding. It looked amazing I can't believe what theypulled off in such a short amount of time. It's more than I could have ever dreamed of.

There are gorgeous flowers everywhere in perfect place. A statue in the middle front behind Xavier who let me tell you looks amazing too.

A/N. Just to give you an idea of what X looks like. No coat though.

He hasn't noticed me yet because he's looking down. But just as I think that he starts to look up and as his eyes met mine it was like the whole world around me melted away. Nothing but right now in this moment mattered. Before I even realized it was happening I was already walking to him withLiza by my side. I couldn't stop the huge smile on my face even if I tried. It seemedlike only seconds and a lifetime before I finally reached him and he took my hand in his.

Xavier was smiling just like me. I've never seen him look so happy.I couldn't be more glade that it's me that cause that amazing smile to make an appearance. The ceremony was beginning as everyone took their seats.

Xavier pulled me close and whispered in my ear, "I love you."I leaned into him and whispered back "I love you too.""Good." He said as he pulled back and began saying his vows.

"Gidget, I know I haven't been there for you when you needed me most .But I hope to make up for that everyday for the rest of my life. I've never felt about anyone the way I do for you. I love you and I will do everything in my power to protect you and love you all I can."

His beautiful vows had brought a tear to my eye but I hadn't noticed until he gently whipped it off with his thumb.

"No more tears for me."

I smile at him and start my vows.

"Even though we didn't start off on the best of terms I've never been happier than with you. I love you and I can't imagine my life without you now that I have you in it and I wouldn't want to. I hope to spend the rest of my days with you because I know if I do then I'm happy."

Xavier leaned into kiss me passionately on the lips. I've never felt more loved than in this moment.

He pulled back and said, "Time for the marking, are you ready?"

I nodded my head and he turned his head so I could mark him first.Fangs out I leaned in a little hesitant but bit down and let the blood flow down my throat yet again. I felt more connected to him than ever. I stopped and pulled back licking my lips as I did.

He looked into my eyes before leaning into my neck same as I did him except he lightly kissed my neck before plunging his fangs in.He was right it didn't hurt, it felt good like we were finally whole. As happiness Washed over me Xavier pulled back and smiled looking into my eyes.

But then something changed he wasn't smiling he looked sad.I looked to see what was wrong only to find red bleeding though his shirt.It all happened so fast I couldn't process what was happening.He started to fall and I tried to catch him only making my fall to the ground with him.The tears were flowing from my eyes steadily it felt as though my heart had been ripped out.

I looked up only to see Bianca holding his heart in her hands. I couldn't control the rage that came over me as I charged at her but just as I was about to snap her flimsy neck I couldn't go any further.Bianca put her index finger to her lips in a shhh.

And that's the last thing I saw before everything went black.

THE END

Part 2 ~ Chapter 1

G idget's POV:

1 month later

I can't move anything. My whole body feels like it's on fire, and burning from the inside out.I can't remember anything after I saw Bianca.

I looked around to try and figure out where I am.All I can see is concrete but it's hard to tell because it's completely dark.I tried to get up to find a way out but I'm too weak to move.

Then I could almost hear someone talking.It was too quiet so I tried to focus in on it more.

"You can keep her like this you'll kill her." A male voice said."When you agreed to this you knew what you were getting into." A woman said."You never said you were going to kill her!" He yelled.

"You said that you wanted him and I could take her away." "Well maybe I changed my mind.""Really then maybe I need to rethink letting him live.""You wouldn't dare!" She yelled."Try me."He said.

"Fine you can have the stupid girl but I don't want to see her again.""That can be arranged, however you are staying on my property. So you better keep you and you pet one your side." He said.

Those voices sounded familiar but in my current state I could place the faces to the voices.

Until the door opened and light flooded into the room rendering my sight for a moment.

After a second I could make out red hair and an older man.As they came up to me I knew exactly who they were.Bianca and none other than Victor.

But that doesn't make sense why does he want me alive?And that means that Xavier is alive because he said he let him live.

But if he's alive why can't I feel him?Is he hurt?How is he alive?

I have all these questions and no way to answer them.

I start to tremble in fear at the thought of what will happen to me.With the little strength I had left I tried to drag myself away but to no avail.They kept coming closer to me.

"Well look who decided to wake up." Bianca said.

Victor came closer and asked, "can you move any?"

He almost sounded worried but I knew better than that.Victor isn't capable of something like caring.But how is he alive and what will he do to me now that he has me?

"I suppose I'll leave you and the girl since she's yours now." She said as she shut the door.

"Here drink." He said.

There's no way I'm drinking that.

"You do realize that you can really move so you'll drink even if you don't want too."

"Look I know you have no reason to trust me but I am here to help you." He said.

Now I'm more confused than before. Is he trying to play some sick mind game on me? The blood from the bag he's holding trickled down my throat. I could feel me gaining the use of my limbs back. The constant pain finally fading away.

I gained enough strength to move away from him. I went to the corner of the room.

"What did he do to you?" He said surprised. "Who?" I choked out. "Victo r." "But your..... you ... what?" I could process what he was trying to say.

"Oh! You don't know?" He stepped closer to me. "Know what?" "Victor had an identical twin, and that's me. I'm your uncle. My name is Emmet." He said.

"I ..... I don't believe you." I said with a shaky voice.

"I know, but hopefully someday you will." He said.

He started to go to the door but turned around to face me.

"Well are you coming?" "Where?" "Out of this cell and to a decent room."

I followed to get out of this horrible concrete room. He lead me down a long hall and to the right. Then into the second door on the right. We walked inside and I couldn't believe my eyes.

The room was almost as big as the one at Xavier's. It had 2 large windows with sapphire blue drapes hanging at the side. The whole room was sapphire and black things with a queen sized bed.It was so pretty and I couldn't possibly understand why he had brought me here.Maybe it's a mistake. I looked over to him with wide eyes, but I noticed something.

Victor had brown eyes but Emmet has on blue eye and one brown.He also has a large scar over his left eye. There were some other small details that made them very different too but I'm still skeptical.

"What's wrong? Do you not like the room.... cause I can get you another one or you can pick out whatever you want for it," he started to ramble on but I stopped him.

"No the room is great, it's beautiful. I'm just not really sure why you brought me here."

"This is your room now, why else?"

I pointed to myself and asked, " Me?"

He nodded.

I took another look around the room and then I decided to test the uncle thing.

"Can I ask you something?"

"Anything."

"Where's Xavier?" I asked.

"He's here."

"Is he okay?"

"Yes."

"Can I see him?"

"No. I'm sorry you can't."

"But he's my mate and if he's okay I want to see him."

"You can't Bianca won't allow it and if you do she will take you away again and I can't risk that." He said in panic.

"Why do you care? You've never even met me." I said with tears in my eyes.

"I care because I'm your father and I can't lose you again! Not again!" He said in devastation.

"But... you said you weren't Victor."

"I'm not."

"Then how are you my father?"

"I will explain it all to you one day but for now you need to rest."

He left the room and I went over to the bed in pure exhaustion.It only took a moment for the darkness to take over.

Chapter 2

When I woke up I felt better than before but still not great. I feel disgusting because I haven't had a shower in god knows how long.I got up and looked around the room and I found the bathroom and walked in.There was a new toothbrush and toothpaste, so I did my morning routine.

When I looked into the mirror I didn't even recognize the girl staring back at me.My under eyes were sunken and dark. My face was slim and colorless.I was much paler than normal. There was no life in my eyes. I was about to take a shower until I realized I didn't have any clean clothes.

I walked back into the room hoping that there was some clothes some-where.I found some drawers where there were under garments.That weird enough were the right size. I finally found the closet that was filled with clothes.I couldn't believe my eyes I've never seen so many clothes.I quickly shuffled through and found the most comfy looking clothes which was sweat pants a crop top and matching sweater.(Outfit at the top.)I went back and took my shower.

When I was don't I brushed my hair and braided it.When I came out I wasn't sure if I should leave the room or not.I mean I don't know where to go in this huge place.But then again I can't stay in this room forever.I slowly approached the door and turned the knob.

I peered into the hallway trying to decide which way to go.I decided to go right. So I walked down the long dark hallway.Until I heard someone talking.

"Take this to Emmet." Bianca said."Okay." He said."And be quick, you can't be over there long." She said.

The voice was one I thought I'd never hear again. I couldn't help the tear that stained my face form the sound.I quickly ran the opposite way so Bianca wouldn't catch me.His step grew close and I started to panic.Why hadn't he come to get me?Did he change his mind?

I was too lost in my thoughts to notice that he was right in front of me.I gazed into his blue eyes but they weren't the same.It was like there was nothing behind them not love like before.

"Xavier." I breathed out."Gidget." He said with no emotion."You're alive ?""Obviously.""Why didn't you look for me?""Because I don't want you."

He pushed past me and walked on like nothing happened.I slowly walked to my room but as soon as the door shut I lost it.I dropped to the floor with a constant stream of tears from my eyes. It felt like someone had ripped my heart out and stomped it.Someone had rushed to my side and pulled me into their arms.

"What's wrong Gidget?" Emmet said.

"What happened? Are you hurt?"I shook me head."He...he just." I couldn't finish the sentence."You saw Xavier." He said in realization."Oh, I'm so sorry Gidget." He said as he held me closer.

I must have fallen asleep while crying because I woke up in my bed.I looked around and saw two blood bags with a note by them.

Gidget you need to drink before you get any weaker.I hope type O is okay for you.~ Emmet

I guess Emmet doesn't know that I can't drink those.I get up and take the bags in my hand.I guess I'll try to find where they keep these.

I finally navigate through the house to what looks like a kitchen.Looking for a fridge someone snuck up on me making me jump and almost drop the blood.I turn quickly to find Emmet.

"You need to eat Gidget." He said."I know but I can't eat that.""We have other types. What do you like?""No I can't have it at all. I need vampire blood all the other makes me throw up."He looked surprised. "Oh, um well I can give you some blood.""Really?""Sure."

He looked around and grabbed a knife from the counter.He slit his wrist and held it out to me.I looked to him and he nodded so I took his wrist and put it to my lips.After awhile I felt him pull back so I released him.

I looked up to him and said, "Thank you.""You're welcome. Now you better go rest again.""But I've slept most of the day.""That's okay. You've been through a lot."I nodded. "Okay goodnight Emmet.""Goodnight Gidget."

I went back to my room. Not really sleepy so I went over to the window and looked outside. It was getting pretty dark out.I looked around the room and saw a bookshelf.On it there was Jane eyre. I picked it up and went to reading.Shortly after I fell asleep yet again.

Chapter 3

It's been a week and I haven't seen Xavier since that day. In all honesty I don't think I could take another run in like that. I just want toUnderstand what happened. How can he be in love on moment and not even a little bit the next.

He doesn't want me.

That's all I could seem to think about. He just got me and he doesn't want me. The cold eyes I looked into are not theeyes I fell in love with. The kind, resilient, amazing blue eyes are the ones I love.But those cold, cruel, and dull eyes I saw belong to a completely different person.It's like he just flipped a switch somewhere and became someone else.

Did I do something wrong?

What happened while I was unconscious?

Did he choose Bianca over me?

...

Completely lost in my thoughts I hadn't even noticed that someone came into my room.I heard someone awkwardly clear their throat and turned around instantly.When I did my eyes were met with Emmets.

"I wanted to come and check on you. I knocked a few times but you never responded." He said. " it's fine and I'm okay thanks." I said looking down at my hands.

"No you're not, you've been eating well and should be doing better than this. You pale and weak and losing weight. It's only been a little while the toll of losing a mate shouldn't be this much. I worried you won't make it much longer.I just got you and I can't take losing you." At the end his voice began to crack.

"I'm sorry. I don't know what's happening to me. I just feel numb and I don't know what to do about it." I said in a panic.

Emmet came closer and held me close.

"I don't know what to do either." He said softly.

Shortly after he left my room.

I did it know what to do so I left my room to explore the grounds some.I walked outside of the mansion to go to the gardens. When I finally found it I couldn't believe it.It's even more beautiful than Xavier's... my mind once again drifted to him.I'm not sure what the laws are here but is there, divorce? So many things don't make sense to me right now and I fear that won't change.I could hear talking from in the garden so I tried to make out what they were saying.

"You spoke to her!" Bianca said."Yes but don't worry I only told her that I don't want her." Xavier said.

She moved closer to him with a smirk and said into his ear, "Well at least you did something right."

A pain shot through my chest as the proceeded to kiss.I could bare to watch. So I did what I do best I ran away hoping the hurt would stop.Tears streamed down my face as I ran out of breath, to weak to continue.Looking around i can barely see all the trees through the darkness.I don't know how I could get this far away I barely ran any.

I hear a limb snap in the distance behind me.I turned but it was too late and the thing had already lunged at me.I scream in agony as the claws tear through my skin.Yellow eyes is the last thing I saw before darkness overcame the pain.

Right when the attack happened

Emmet's POV:

I was searching for Gidget when I heard the scream.My heart started to pound with fear because I knew it was her.I ran as fast as I could in the direction of the scream.I could faintly make out the silhouette of the beast as I approached.And I know exactly what it is.Unfortunately however he ran off before I got there and I was too worried about Gidget to care.

"Gidget... Gidget, come on just open your eyes. Please." I begged as I held her lifeless body in my trembling arms.

I picked her up carrying her to the house and yelling for them to fetch the doctors.As I entered Xavier was standing there with Bianca smiling.He turned and gaze upon the torn and tattered Gidget.The smile fell into a sorrow I've never seen before.He should feel bad for her though, he shouldn't feel anything for her.

I hurried with her to the doctors and they instantly took over.People were all around her. They were about to give her blood when I had to stop them.

"Stop! She can't have that." I yelled making them freeze."Then what does she drink?" A Doctor asked."Vampire Blood.""Can you give her some?"I nodded in response.

It seemed like hours had passed before the doctors finally came out of the room.

"How is she?" I asked."She's stable for now but the blood still isn't giving her the nourishment she needs to survive.""How long does she have?""Maybe the night. We have nothing else to try. I'm sorry.""I have something else." I said as I rushed off.

I walked up to the door and knocked.After a moment someone opened the door.

"Hello Xavier..."

Chapter 4

Emmets POV:

"What are you doing here?" Xavier asked.

"I need your help with something." I said as I looked into his eyes pleading.

He looked around as if not wanting to get caught then asked, "With what?"

"Gidget isn't doing well, they don't think she'll make it through the night."

Something changed in his eyes but soon was masked with another emotion.

"What does that have to do with me?"

I don't know if he's playing dumb or something is wrong with him.

I look at him confused, "You know she can't live without you."

"She has done fine so far."

"If she was doing fine I wouldn't be here right now, you are her last option."

He looked as if he didn't know how to reply.

"Just come with me and see for yourself."

He looked unsure at first but then walked out with me.We made our way down the hall and as we got closer to Gidget the more fidgety Xavier seemed to be. I think that even if he doesn't realize it he can still sense her.Maybe he's not hopeless after all.

We entered the room and Gidget was lying there looking almost lifeless.I looked to Xavier and saw all the life drain from his face.I was almost as if something clicked and he knew exactly what to do.He rushed to her bite his wrist and put it up to her mouth.The longer it took the hope we had started to fade.I saw a lone tear fall from his eyes and that's when I knew whatever Bianca did to him, at that moment wasn't working.

"Please," he pleaded holding her tight against him.

And then,

Gidget's POV:

I felt warmth all around me. I'm not sure why but felt safe.I slowly started to open my eyes. The room was so bright I winced a little.Someone was holding me but not Emmet because I could see him across the room.I looked up and saw the face I had been craving for all this time.But why is he here, I thought he didn't care any more.While I was lost in thought I must have moved because he realized I was awake.

"Thank God." Xavier said as he moved closer to kiss me.

Before I knew it his lips where on mine and I lost all train of thought and melted into the kiss. When it finally broke I looked into those blue eyes I loved so much.I put my hand on his face and he leaned into my touch.

"Why?" I said in a soft voice.

"I didn't have control." He looked down in shame.

"How's that possible?"

"I'll explain everything later right now you need to rest."

"No! I want to know now. I've been horrible this whole time and you didn't care at all and I need to know why!" I said as I moved away from him.

He looked to me and slightly nodded.

"Well you know how Bianca took my heart out?"

I nodded urging him to continue.

"She kept it. I don't know who did the spell but a witch made it to where she can control me with my heart. I didn't realize what had happened until the moment I saw you looking almost dead. I don't know how but it broke me out of the daze I was in."

" Do you know where she has it?"

"Last I knew she had it in her room, other than that no."

"We need to get it back."

"We do not need to. I need to. I can't risk you getting hurt again."

"You think I'm going to let you go when she may still be able to control you then you are beyond insane."

"Fine, but if she's there we leave right away, and we are not doing it until you rest for a little."

As much as I wanted to object I felt the exhaustion from everything pulling at me.So I nodded and leaned back.

"You'll stay right?" I said not wanting to leave him again.

"I wouldn't leave for anything." He said taking my hand in his.

Emmet came closer to me and leaned down to kiss my forehead.

"I'm so happy you're okay, I'll see you later alright."

"Okay."

Emmet headed for the door and gave one last glance before closing the door behind him. I looked to Xavier before falling into a deep sleep.

Chapter 5

Emmet's POV:

I walked out of the room and headed down the hall. It's far too risky for them to do this by themselves. They have already done so much to be together. I need to do this.For her, I've already missed so much. I just want her to be happy and he makes her happy. If it comes to it I can handle Bianca by myself just fine.

I found her room and went inside quickly. It was very tidy more than I expected.I looked around in the obvious places, under the bed and such.Looking around running out of time and spaces to check. Then I glanced at the table near the door. Her purse. I shrug not like she's know for being the brightest.I rushed over to check when I heard the door knob turn. Quickly I rushed behind the door and peaked into the purse. Sure enough Xavier's heart was in there.

I grabbed it and went into a fighting position, ready for whatever is behind that door. But who came out wasn't what I expected.

"Winter!" I said surprised.She put her finger to her lips. "Shh."

She grabbed my arm and pulled me behind her into a nearby room.

"What are you doing here?" I asked."When Bianca came to me for the spell but refused to tell me whose heart it was I knew something was wrong. However I don't know how you come into this." She said.

I explained everything that had happened to her. She looked absolutely heartbroken.

"I never would have left if I knew this would be the result." She said looking down."Winter it's not your fault you did the best you could." I said.She nodded. "Where are they?""I'll take you." I said leading the way.

Gidget's POV:

As I woke up I noticed Xavier staring intently at me.

"Hi" I said snapping him out of the daze.He smiled and moved closer. "Feeling better?""I feel great." I smiled back.

Xavier leaned into kiss me but the door interrupted us.We both looked but I didn't believe my eyes.

"Winter." I whispered.

"Gidget." She's said as she came close to me but I moved closer to Xavier. She seemed to get the hint because she stopped.

"I deserve that." She nodded."Why are you here?"

She told us she was the one who cast the spell & she knew something wasn't right.

"Wait you got his heart?" I said surprised.Emmet nodded."Then we can put it back, right?""Well we need one thing to do that.""What?""Bianca's blood."

"No problem." I started to get up but felt a hand on my shoulder."Where are you going?" Xavier said."To get some blood of course." I said.He shook his head. "It's too dangerous.""Actually right now she the least expected. She stands the best chance." Winter said.

Xavier and Emmet looked at each other and nodded.

"Fine." They both sighed."Well I need to change." I said heading to my room.

When I got there I changed (outfit at the top) and went towards Bianca's room.I got the I could hear her rummaging through her room and quietly cursing.I knock on the door and wait. She opened shortly after.

She narrowed her eyes when she spotted me. "You. What do you want?""Are you okay?" She looked like a mess."I'm fine.""Shame." I said as the anger boiled up in me.

She looked at me with wide eyes not expecting that. I came forward fast and kneed her in the stomach.As she hunched forward I slammed her head against the door frame.She was out like a light. I smiled, grabbed her foot and drug her to the room with the others.When I got there everyone looked at me weirdly.

"What?" I asked."That was fast." Emmet said."Didn't take much." I shrugged.

Unlike the others Xavier smirked at me almost proud looking.Winter went to Bianca and slit her wrist to get enough blood.Then continued to do the spell as I went over to Xavier.

"So where it that come from?" He whispered in my ear."She got on my nerves way to many times." I said looking up at him.He turned back to winter pulling me close to him.

"Okay the spell is removed however putting it in will still be painful.""O kay, that's fine." He nodded.

She came closer and I moved away so she could do it. Winter took the heart and put it close to his chest then with one fluid motion put it back in. Xavier clutched his chest and fell to his knees.I moved next to him and held him close trying to do what I could to stop the pain.

"It's not stopping." He said through clenched teeth."Gidget he's going to need to drink your blood. It with strengthen the bond and help him heal." Winter stated.

I nodded and moved closer to him pulling my hair to the side.He gave me a worried look but I put my hand on his shoulder to reassure him.Leaning close I felt his fangs pierce my skin as a sense of bliss overcame me.He pulled me closer as he drank more before slowly pulling away and looking into my eyes. Winter came to me with a washcloth to get the blood off but Xavier took it and did it for me. We then looked to Emmet and Winter.

"So what do we do with Bianca now?" I asked.

"I know just the place." Emmet said with a smile.